Kindness is

by Michaela Castillo

Copyright © 2025 Michaela Castillo.
All rights reserved. No part of this publication may be reproduced, distributed, or transmitted in any form without the prior permission of the publisher.

ISBN: 9798305771602 (Paperback)

"I've learned that people will forget what you said. People will forget what you did. But people will never forget how you made them feel" - Maya Angelou.

Dedication

To my three beautiful girls. I am a better person everyday, because of you.
With all my love, Mom xxx

Kindness is

by Michaela Castillo

Kindness is
patience when someone is slow,

It's showing you're willing to learn and to grow.

Patience is Kindness

It's saying "I'm sorry" spoken, soft and kind,

To calm the storm and ease the mind.

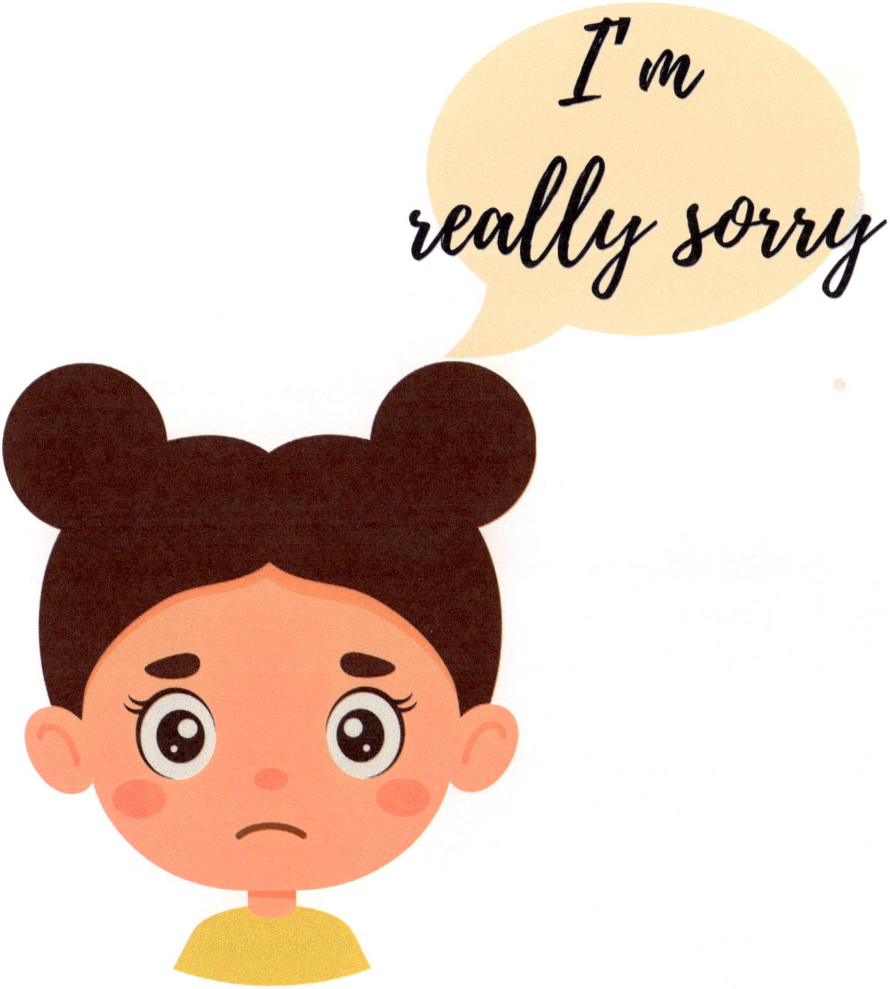
I'm
really sorry

Kindness is
laughter that fills up the air,

A quiet moment of love that you share.

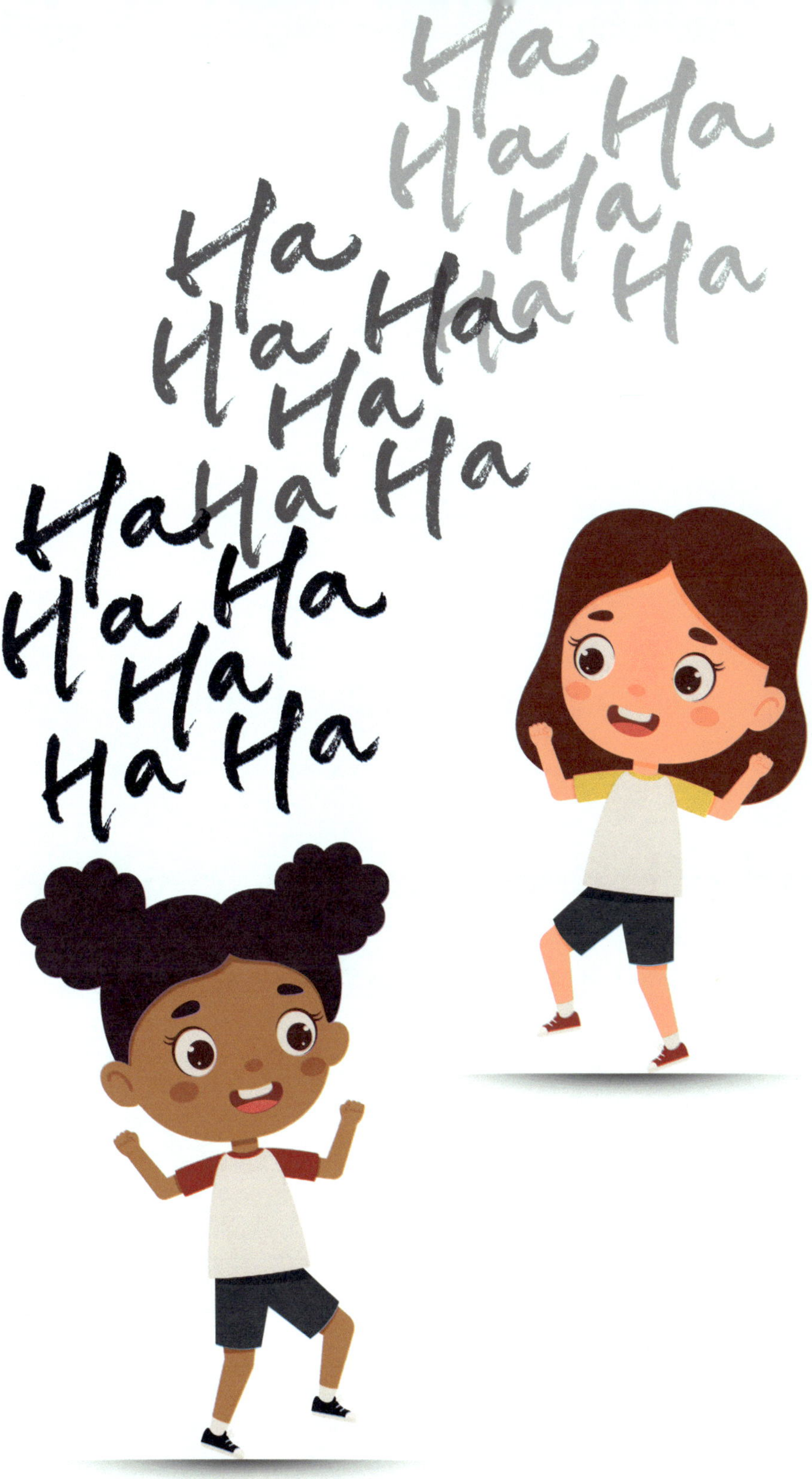

Ha
Ha Ha
Ha
Ha Ha
Ha
Ha Ha
Ha
Ha
Ha Ha
Ha Ha
Ha
Ha Ha

It's standing by someone
who's feeling alone,

And offering comfort, a warm
safe home.

Koala-ty Hugs

Kindness is forgiving when someone makes a mistake,

It's giving a gift, for the joy it will make.

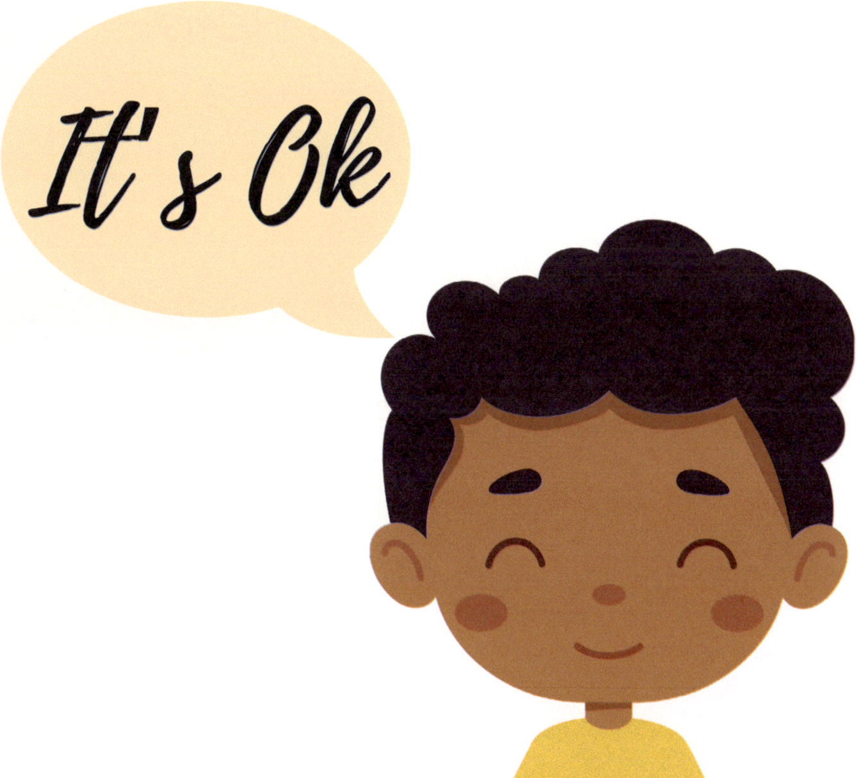
It's Ok

It's the thoughtfulness shown with a simple "please,"

And caring for others with heartfelt ease.

"Would you like a doughnut?"

"Yes Please"

Kindness is
giving without asking for
much,

It's a soft, gentle whisper, a
sweet loving touch.

You're my best friend

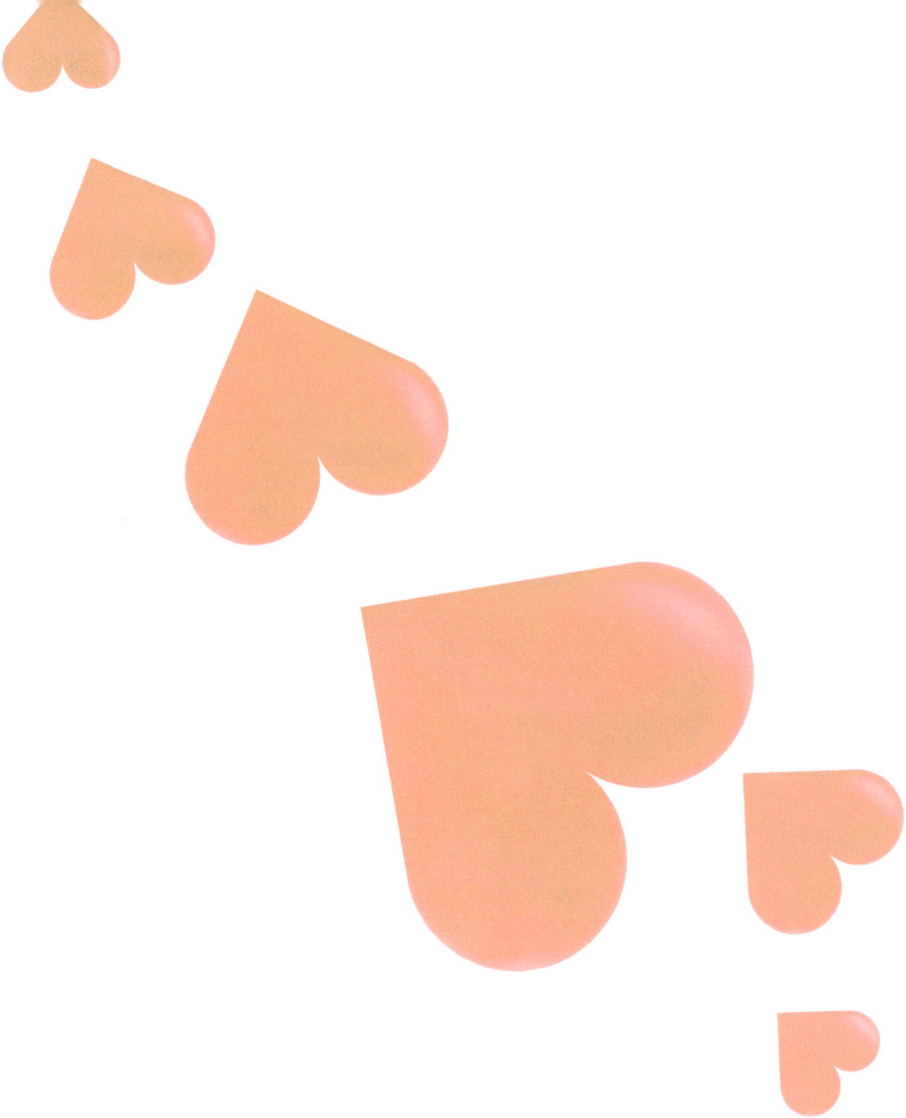

It's seeing the good in everyone you meet,

And spreading a love that's calm and sweet.

Kindness is
seeing beyond your own heart

and sharing warmth wherever you start.

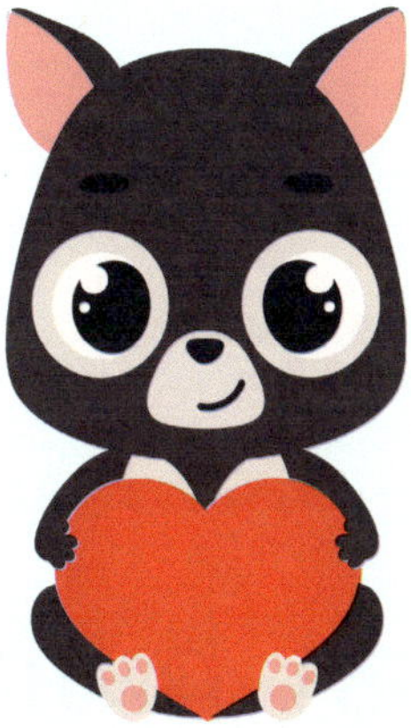

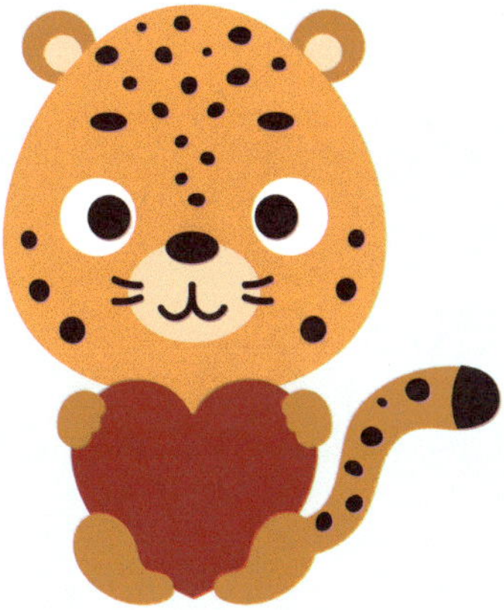
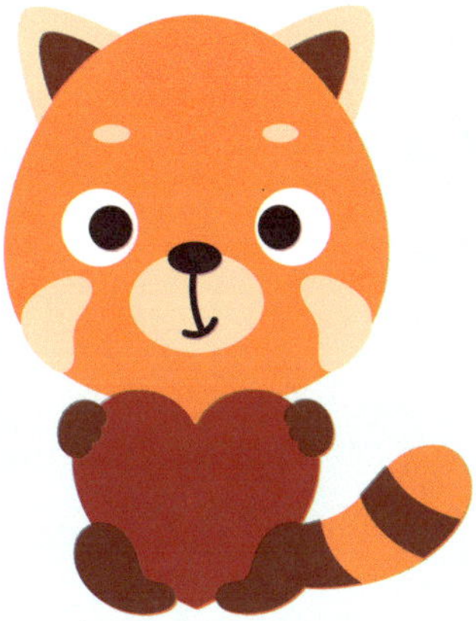
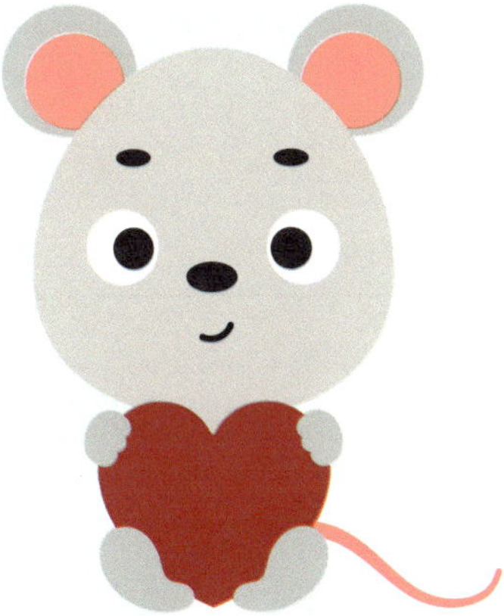
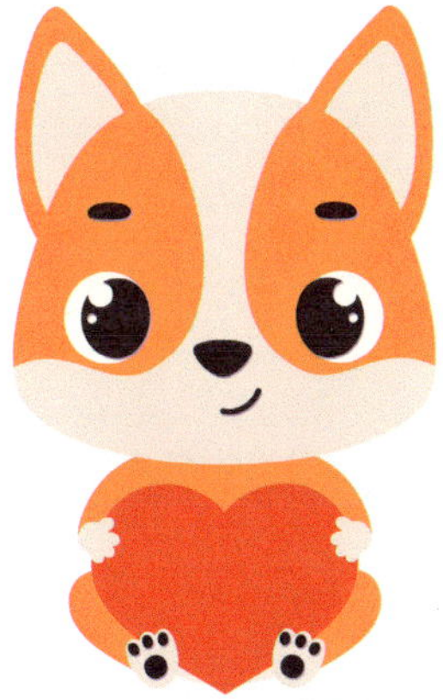

It's in every action, both big and small.

Kindness is..

simply caring for all.

Ready to lend a trunk

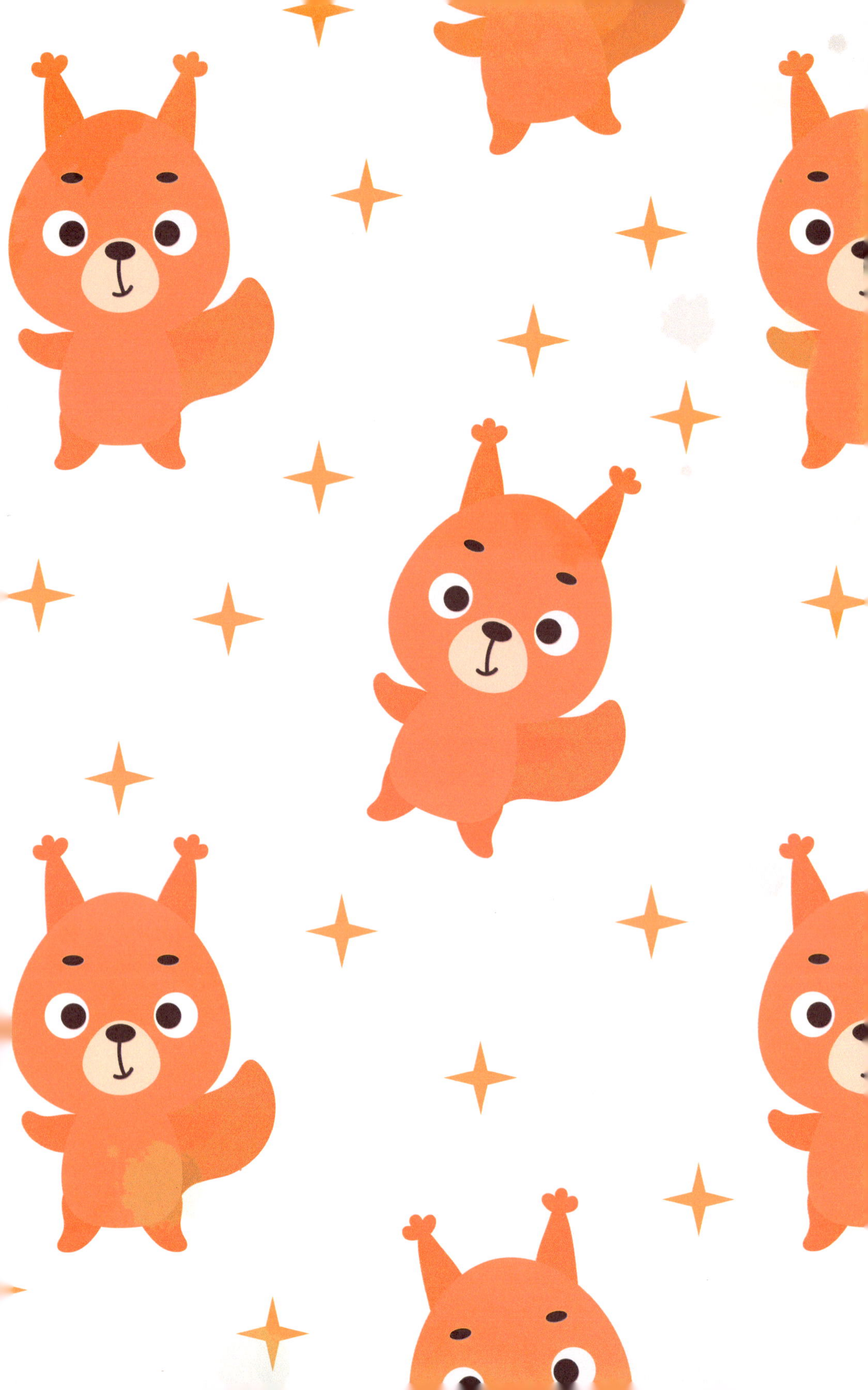

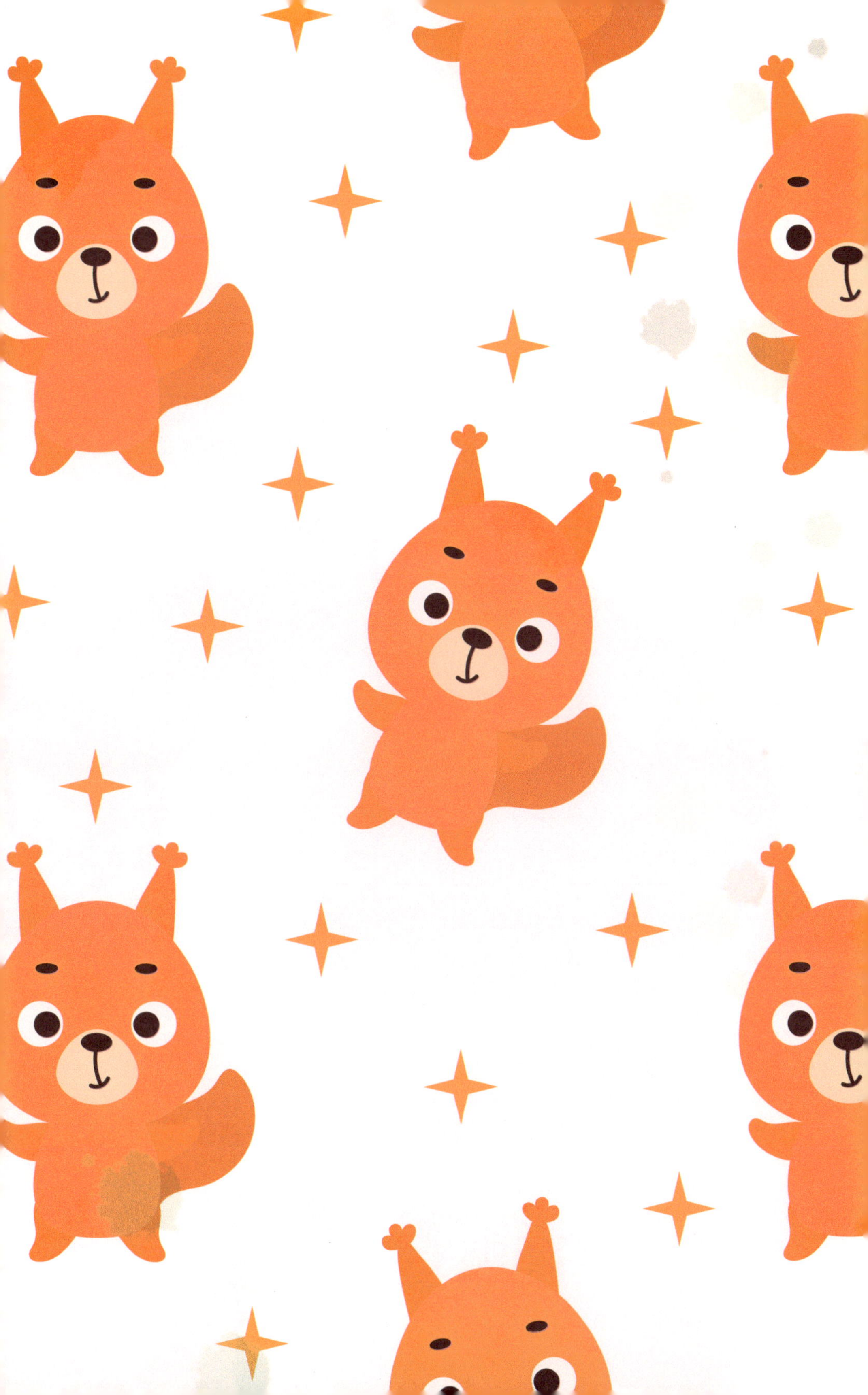

Made in the USA
Columbia, SC
18 February 2025